CW00853782

SURVIVAL

A TALE OF COURAGE AND HOPE

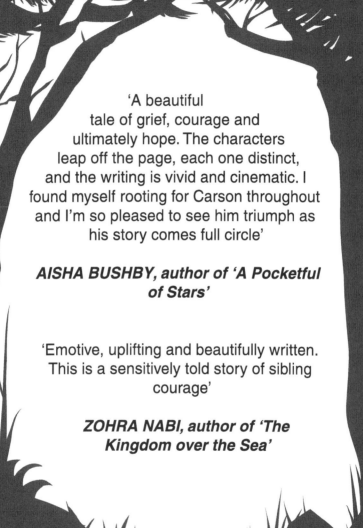

'A beautiful tale of grief, courage and ultimately hope. The characters leap off the page, each one distinct, and the writing is vivid and cinematic. I found myself rooting for Carson throughout and I'm so pleased to see him triumph as his story comes full circle'

AISHA BUSHBY, author of 'A Pocketful of Stars'

'Emotive, uplifting and beautifully written. This is a sensitively told story of sibling courage'

ZOHRA NABI, author of 'The Kingdom over the Sea'

First published in Great Britain in 2023 by Aspire Publishing.

This paperback edition first published in 2023.

Second Edition 2023.

Text copyright © 2023 A. Moti S. Moti K. Hassam

Illustrations copyright © 2023 Jogia Design & Shriya Patel

All rights reserved. No part of this publication may be reproduced, stored in a retrieval system, or transmitted in any form or any means, electronic, mechanical, photocopying, recording or otherwise, without the prior permission of the publisher and copyright owner.

Aspire Publishing,
Leicester, United Kingdom

A CIP catalogue record for this book is available from the British Library

This book is a work of fiction. Names, characters and incidents are used fictitiously. Any resemblance to actual people, living or dead, events or locales is entirely coincidental.

PB ISBN 978-1-3999-5682-6

SURVIVAL

A.MOTI   **K.HASSAM**   **S.MOTI**

Aspire Publishing

CONTENTS

PROLOGUE

He slumps back against the bark of a tree. He has no choice now. His eyes are stinging from exhaustion, or is it from crying? Does it matter? He's near the end now. He doesn't want to continue. He can't continue. He'll be meeting his mum soon. He shuts his eyes and lets the black cloud overwhelm him. Take over. Engulf him. He sinks deeper and deeper into the dark nothingness. He clutches his medal tightly and remembers his mum. He prays for his dad. He takes one last look at his sister's sleeping face. Her trusting face. A sharp pain of guilt stabs at his heart. His mum's dying wish was that he protect his sister at all costs.

How can he give up now? But how can he carry on when he doesn't know where he is going? Just then, from the corner of his eyes, he notices Isla's eyes open slightly, give him a comforting smile, squeeze him tightly and then drift back to sleep. That was the push Carson needed to continue. He could do this. He could do this for Isla. He could do this for his mum.

FLASHBACKS

The dreams hadn't stopped. Would they ever stop? Did Carson want them to stop?

GOAL!!! Carson had scored a tremendous goal which put his team in the lead! He looked at his mother, whose golden locks were gleaming in the sun, and as usual her lively smile was painted across her face. His best friend, Theodore, jumped on him like a bear and roared triumphantly,

"You did it! I knew I could count on you!"

A rush of emotions coursed through Carson like racing cars. He had done it for his team. He was the reason that his team were able to celebrate. He sighed contentedly, hoping it would be one of many proud moments. A few seconds later, his mum was by his side as he received the jewel-encrusted medal reading; "Man of the Match 2016". As Carson glanced at his mum, he could see her face shining with excitement. She was ready to burst with pride and Carson knew he would never forget the look on her face.

Moments later, Carson was thrashing around in his bed, while subconsciously rubbing his temple as if to rid himself from his frequent nightmares.

Then, suddenly a whirring noise lingered while a collage of purple, blue and teal appeared as if Carson was being hypnotised. He was now in the living room, reading his favourite book, Harry Potter. His mother walked into the room, limping. Carson knew something was wrong as recently he often walked in on his mum and dad exchanging worried, desperate whispers. His mum's mystery condition appeared to worsen daily. It seemed as if she was as thin as a twig now and her once fine, golden locks were now grey like dull, sombre clouds. Worry engulfed him, as every day she got worse and worse until Carson made a life changing promise to his mother to always protect his little sister, Isla.

He continued thrashing around restlessly in his bed and he was now in a place with bright lights and white walls. A flurry of beeping sounds echoed from around. A hospital. A pained look adorned his face mixed with confusion, as tears formed in his eyes. He tried to be brave, however he had had unspeakable visions of something he feared might happen. He never lost hope, not now, not ever. Without warning, a very piercing, sharp beep filled the room in one long syllable.

"Time of death, 2.43am."

Then silence.

Carson didn't realise it at the time, but this was the day he lost both of his parents, along with a part of himself.

Coldness crept up on Carson while he switched over to his right, then left side. Abruptly, he sat up in his bed, gasping. Panting heavily and covered in sweat, he grabbed at his head; he couldn't handle these vivid flashbacks. Absentmindedly, he switched on his side lamp and with his dull, lifeless eyes, he stared at the frame on his bedside table of his mother. Carson knew he wasn't coping, but he also knew he had no choice, so he wiped the sweat from his forehead, inhaled deeply to steady his breath and got out of bed. 6.55am. It was nearly time for Isla to wake up and he hadn't sorted out her packed lunch yet.

JUST ANOTHER DAY

As Carson rolled out of bed, he ignored the dull headache brewing – no doubt the result from his restless night. He lumbered out of the room and called 'goodbye' to his dad as he heard the front door slam shut. He sighed inwardly, then fixed a smile onto his face before knocking on Isla's door.

"Wake up sleepy head," he called through the gap in her bedroom door.

"I'm sleeping," yawned Isla, dramatically scrunching up her eyes.

"I've put a 5 minutes snooze alarm on Miss Sass - I'll see you downstairs when it rings." He shook his head, as a smile played at the corner of his lips.

Traipsing downstairs, Carson made a mental note of the order in which he would sort the morning routine: make Isla's packed lunch, fill her water bottle (which of course must be the unicorn one), and lastly, start on her breakfast before quickly throwing something together for himself.

"Carson....!" Isla bellowed at the top of her lungs,

"Where is my cardigan?"

"In your left side cupboard, top shelf and yes princess, I've ironed it already," Carson replied while muttering, "Honestly that girl would lose her head if it wasn't screwed on."

Moments later, Isla was sitting at the kitchen table scoffing down her bowl of cheerios, which was waiting for her. Without a care in the world, she gazed out of the window, animatedly telling Carson all about her swimming lesson, which was due that evening.

"I've nearly passed Stage 2 Carson. Will you buy me the certificate if I do it today?" she asked, knowing full well that he wouldn't refuse her.

"Let's just see how you get on this evening, shall we?"

Breakfast time finished, and as usual, it was the expected morning rush of getting out of the house. Carson switched lights off as he swept through the hallway and kitchen, collecting Isla's bits and bobs on his way, while Isla fussed over which shoes to wear. She always chose the dreaded pink, glitter boots in the end, however Carson smiled at her and told her how beautiful she looked. Finally, making their way outside, Isla noticed the dark grey cloud painted across the sky.

"It's a 5-minute walk missy, you'll be fine. It's not even raining yet," Carson replied as he cajoled his sister forward.

Isla wouldn't budge. She sighed and turned to Carson with a sombre look overtaking her once playful demeanour.

"Is mummy angry with us?"

Carson had to catch his breath. He often thought about his mother, but Isla rarely mentioned her. He wasn't sure if it was because she didn't remember mum much or if it was because Isla knew that Carson didn't want to talk about her; either way, mum was rarely mentioned. He gulped and inhaled deeply.

"What makes you say that?" he asked, while rubbing Isla's shoulder comfortingly.

Isla heaved another sigh and looked down, biting her lip.

"Well... well... once... when it was really sunny, you... you said that mummy loved us and that she was happy in heaven." Isla was fidgeting with the corner of her cardigan.

"It's too grey today," she continued.

Carson's throat clogged up. He couldn't speak. He wanted to comfort his sister, to protect her like he always did, but in that moment, he couldn't speak. He just couldn't. Forcing back tears, he hugged Isla tightly, and muttered that they would be late for school if they didn't hurry up. That was all he could manage.

It was a very silent walk to school that day. The 5-minutes seemed like an eternity and Carson couldn't wait to drop Isla off so he could be alone with his thoughts.

A few moments later, they arrived at the entrance of 'Borkeley Carrol School' and with a sigh of relief, Carson exchanged goodbyes with Isla and made his way to his own school, Crickey Valley High. On the way, he met his friend, Theodore, who was walking with Jeremy. Carson simply said, "Hey Theo, J," and continued walking. He was itching more than ever to be alone with his thoughts. Theo didn't notice any difference in Carson's behaviour. He was used to Carson's quietness now. Theo once mourned the friend that he had 'lost', but now he just accepted the silence as the norm. The Carson who used to jump on him in the mornings and play tricks on him was long gone, but he wouldn't give up on his friend, even if all he got now was a hi.

Carson could hear Theo and Jeremy converse the whole

way to school, and he briefly caught bits of the conversation: Theo had bought a new dog. This once would have filled Carson with excitement, as he always wanted a dog, but he was never allowed due to his mum's allergy to dogs, however today, hearing this news made no difference to him. He took a deep breath and was about to make small talk with Theo, but then he bit his lip. He just couldn't. He didn't know what was stopping him from speaking to Theo, but he swallowed, looked down and continued walking.

They were nearly at school and Carson still couldn't get Isla's words out of his head – is mummy angry with us today? He tried to rid his mind of this conversation, lock it away, like he tried to do with all of his uncomfortable thoughts: put it in a drawer to deal with later.

Arriving at school, he glanced up at the vast, ornate building. Although the school was grand, Carson hated it; it was too extravagant for his liking. Too stately. His dad had urged him to make the most of this 'opportunity' and insisted that it was the best school for him. Reluctantly, Carson made his way to the larger building and entered the classroom. Due to the vivid flashbacks from the previous night, he hadn't received a blink of sleep, so he started daydreaming halfway through his first lesson, maths.

"Carson!" thundered Miss Atlas. "You better concentrate as this test won't be forgiving!"

Carson tried to switch his brain on, but he was struggling. Everything seemed a struggle at the moment. The rest of the day passed in a blur.

After what felt like an eternity, Carson left the 'prison' and knew that he just needed to get through the next few hours with Isla and her swimming lesson, before he could return to his solitude back in his bedroom. When he arrived back at Isla's school, he took a deep breath and entered the grounds. Two minutes later, the bell rang and Isla bounded out of the school building, her glitter boots sparkling.

"CARSON!" she bellowed, with a lively smile spreading across her face. "I missed you," she whispered to him, "And look, it's sunny now!" she said pointing at the sky, as her golden locks gleamed in the sun. Carson caught his breath as he found himself thinking about the day in which he won the tournament. A day he would never forget.

"Carson?" Isla moaned, shaking Carson vigorously. He

hadn't realised that he had been daydreaming again. Without saying a word, he gave her a fleeting smile, took Isla's bag from her, held her hand and started walking back home. He tried to erase this constant memory and began to rub at his temple once again. However, he knew his brain was devious, and wasn't forgiving just like that maths test Miss Atlas had reminded him of earlier. He may be able to smile and play with Isla now, but once she was in bed and he was in the confinements of his room, the flashbacks would return. No breaks. No give. They were relentless, unforgiving.

*****

"Carson, what if I don't do it today?" Isla asked, biting on her lip. "I really want my certificate."

Carson shifted closer to her on the wooden bench and gave her a tight squeeze. "I know you will princess, you are an amazing swimmer, and even if you don't today, it doesn't matter – we can try again next week."

"STAGE 2 GROUP!" Kate, Isla's swimming instructor, yelled across the pool.

Isla made her way forward to the edge of the pool and Carson sat back, praying that she would do well. It was her birthday tomorrow and passing would make her day.

As the lesson drew to a close, Kate spoke to Isla and excitement poured out of her as Kate gestured. Climbing out of the pool, she bounded over to Carson; her face radiating with pure joy. There was no trace of the earlier conversation evident on her face – it was simply euphoric.

"I did it, I did it, I did it!" she beamed, while jumping up and down. She could hardly contain herself. "I've passed Carson. Can we go and buy my certificate? Can we go now?" she almost screeched.

Laughing, Carson answered, "Calm down! You need to shower first, but then yes, we can buy it. Well done missy." He started leading her towards the boys changing room.

"Carson, when can I start changing in the girls changing room? The boys one smells."

Carson knew that if his mum was around, Isla wouldn't have ever needed to step foot into the boys changing room. He abruptly caught himself from drifting again and simply replied, "When you are old enough to change yourself missy."

The rest of the evening passed as usual: sorting Isla's swimming bag (put the load of washing on), get the dinner sorted, clean up after dinner, read Isla her bedtime story and tuck her into bed.

Just as Carson finally sat down to do his homework at the dining table, he heard the front door creek open. Briefly looking up, he called, "Hi dad," hoping just for a moment, that his dad would come in and speak to him.

His hope was instantly crushed as his dad called back, "Hey," and went straight upstairs without even popping his head into the dining room. He knew he shouldn't have allowed himself to hope. He heard dad make his way upstairs, then gently knock on Isla's door before entering her bedroom and sitting on the edge of her bed.

"Goodnight," dad whispered, kissing Isla softly on the forehead.

"Daddy! I passed stage 2 – I got my swimming badge!" Isla exclaimed just a little too loudly.

"Ok, we will talk about it tomorrow. You have a big day ahead of you." Dad could see her excitement turn to a frown, but he couldn't give her more than that. He gave Isla one last kiss and left her room, closing the door behind him.

Carson heard the conversation and could picture Isla's disappointment forming on her face – why couldn't dad have just asked her about her badge? He could then hear his dad breathing heavily outside of Isla's room. Was his dad coming down to see him? Carson waited, listening. He heard no noise, so he stood by the bottom of the stairs. He could see dad through the gold-rimmed mirror. Dad was standing at the top of the banister, holding on, as if gripping it for support. Carson leaned in, trying to listen.

Carson watched, as Dad, who was looking up angrily, muttered through clenched teeth, "She needs you, dammit, she needs you!" Dad's voice cracked like a whip, before trembling. Carson had never heard his dad like this. He thought his dad didn't care. Deep down, however, he knew dad was struggling more then he let on.

Carson then noticed dad looking down the stairs, so he moved away from view. He held his breath as he saw his dad standing still for another couple of minutes. Then dad began to make his way downstairs, before sighing and going to his bedroom, closing the door firmly behind him. This was how every day ended for the last 2 years, 3 months and 4 days.

As the bedroom door shut, it slammed on Carson's hope. He sighed and went back to the dinning table, back to his homework.

BIRTHDAY

Isla woke up with a sparkle in her blue eyes and a mischievous smile forming on her face. With a spring in her step, she dashed to the bathroom, grabbed her pink toothbrush and started to hum 'happy birthday' to herself, whilst brushing her teeth. Still humming happy birthday, Isla raced to Carson's room, slammed open the door, which banged hard against the wall, and jumped on him, shaking him vigorously.

"Carson! Carson! Wake up – it's my birthday!"

With an abrupt snort, Carson jolted up and stared at Isla with piercing eyes. He glanced over to his alarm clock.

"Isla, sweetie, its 5:30 in the morning. You've probably woken up the entire street!" he whispered to her, whilst giving her a peck on the forehead.

"But it's my birthday!" whined Isla.

"Just go to bed for one more hour, then we can open your presents together," yawned Carson, rubbing his eyes. "Happy Birthday princess," he continued. "Now off you go."

Silently, Isla made her way out of Carson's room and

shut the door gently behind her.

Once she had shut the door, Isla tiptoed quietly down the stairs, making sure to miss the third step (which had a tendency to creak) and made her way towards the living room. When she entered, she gasped as she found herself in what seemed to be unicorn heaven. Her eyes widened as she stared in admiration at the unicorn balloon, which stood out the most from all of the decorations. Printed on the balloon, was an elegant portrait of a unicorn; it had a rainbow coloured mane with blue, yellow and purple painted across its back and the horn protruding out from its brilliant white skin. Next to it, on the table, were many party bags stuffed to the brim with sweet delicacies such as: coconut coated marshmallows, a variety of pick and mix sweets - including love hearts, strawberry laces and Haribos, and Isla's personal favourite, sugar glazed donuts. Her mouth started to water. Continuing to soak in the atmosphere, she gazed at the pink banner reading, 'Happy 5th Birthday Isla!'. This was carefully hung over the archway. Isla's pupils widened as she looked around. In the corner of the room, she spotted four decorative cubes filled with what looked like multicoloured water balls, spelling out her name: ISLA. Wow, she thought to herself.

She continued to gaze around the room in awe. She took in every detail of the room as if it revealed itself to her inch by inch. Hanging down from the ceiling, she examined the sparkly-pink, pony-shaped piñata (that she hoped would be filled with her favourite chocolate - dairy milk). Isla longed to smash open the piñata, however she knew for two reasons she shouldn't: it would make too much noise while Carson was sleeping and secondly, she would enjoy it more with her friends, who were coming over to her house later that afternoon for the party.

As she stepped away from the pinata, she continued to immerse herself in her unicorn heaven. All around Isla, were confetti balloons. Without thinking, she touched the balloon with the tip of her finger. Realising what she about to do, she moved herself away from the balloons; bursting the balloons would not be helpful at this time of the morning. Isla heaved a contented sigh and noticed the cocktail of aromas which lingered in the air. Turning her head towards the alluring scent, she was almost hypnotised by the sweet smells of candy and freshly baked cake – she couldn't wait to tuck in. Carson must've baked it before he went to sleep, she mused.

Suddenly, from the corner of her eyes, she caught a glimpse of the vast pile of neatly wrapped presents which were placed next to the window. She was mesmerised. The pile was huge! The pile of gold had been labelled and handwritten by Carson, however read, 'Love From Daddy and Carson'. At once, Isla recognised her brother's handwriting. Carson had made all this effort for her. Her heart soared. He was her favourite person, ever.

Isla peered cautiously at a present that had a big enough hole for her to slip her finger inside and feel around. As she clumsily placed her finger inside the hole, she heard the sounds. Tear. Rip. She hurriedly attempted to hide the present at the bottom of the pile, however, just then, Carson appeared at the door. He tried to wear a frown, but a smile was surfacing.

"Oh, umm... hi, C...Carson," she stammered, clutching the present behind her back.

"Good morning missy. What have you got behind your back?"

Isla's face turned red.

Carson burst out laughing. "Come here princess, Happy

Birthday! I can see that you are full of beans and didn't manage to sleep. I hope you haven't wrecked the place before daddy's had a chance to see it."

"Can I please just open one present while we wait for daddy?" Isla pleaded as if butter wouldn't melt.

Just then, dad appeared at the entrance to the living room.

"Morning Carson, Isla, Happy Birthday baby." He turned to Carson. "What time does the party finish?"

"6:00 pm."

"Ok, be ready for 6:30, I have a surprise for you both." He left before Carson had time to respond.

Carson's heart sank as he watched his dad close the door on him yet again. Dad hadn't noticed all the decorations. He hadn't noticed the pile of presents in the corner. He hadn't noticed the delicacies on the table. He hadn't noticed Carson's efforts.

He hadn't noticed anything. What did Carson expect? His dad hadn't noticed anything for the last 2 years, so why should today be any different?

***

As the school bell rang, children flooded out of the

building like a troop of wild monkeys. Carson glanced at the crowd, searching for Isla. After a short while, the crowd died down and Isla raced towards Carson, beaming and gave him an affectionate hug.

"It's my birthday! It's my birthday!" sang Isla. "Quick! Quick! Let's get going!"

Isla tugged at Carson and dragged him towards the school gates.

Once home, the pair rushed straight upstairs to decide on Isla's outfit for the party.

"Do you want your pink t-shirt and skirt or your rainbow dress?" Carson asked, holding an outfit in each hand. Isla chose her pink glittery t-shirt and skirt, which had sequences scattered all over. Once the birthday girl had got dressed, Carson did her hair into two neatly plated french braids, fixing them with golden bows. Isla glanced at herself in the mirror and a smile crossed her face.

"I love it Carson – thank you!"

***

Moments later, the doorbell rang and Isla's friends jostled into the house greeting her and giving her more presents. Her eyes sparkled at the shining boxes in hunger.

"Can we do presents first?" Isla exclaimed in excitement, bouncing on the balls of her feet.

"Woah, calm down missy, let's play with your friends first," replied Carson. "They've just arrived."

"Can we do the piñata first, then?" Isla asked, still jumping up and down.

"Sure."

Without waiting for Carson, Isla declared that she would go first, led her friends into the living room, picked up the bat and wacked the piñata with all her force. Her best friends Chloe, Rachel, Daphne, and Hannah all fought over who would go next, but Carson soon stepped in and the order was set. When it was Hannah's turn, she glared at the pinata with a fierce determination, hitting it as hard as she could. She knocked the foot of the unicorn pinata, which was now half hanging off, causing a shower of sweets to explode over her. She was elated. The girls scrambled like monkeys trying to grab as many sweets as they could.

***

The rest of the party ran smoothly and all of the girls had a great time. Carson knew the party was a success by the constant stream of giggles and squeals that filled the air.

It was almost 6pm. Carson was exhausted – it was hard work entertaining and solely looking after five 5-year olds for 2 hours! Within five minutes, the girls' parents arrived, thanked Carson for the invite, wished Isla a Happy Birthday and ushered their hyper, sugar filled girls out of the house.

The house was once again empty. Carson slumped down on the corner sofa and heaved a sigh of relief. Isla had had an amazing birthday. He had done his mum proud. He reminisced about his fifth birthday when his mum had created Jurassic World in their living room for his party. He remembered the little dinosaur figurines scattered all over the table. He remembered the dinosaur welcome sign, which hung up in the arch of the hallway. He remembered the huge dinosaur shaped balloon which dominated the bay window like a Christmas Tree. He remembered it all. His mum had always gone over and above for his special day and he wanted to make Isla feel the same joy and magic that he did. He looked out of the window towards the sky and smiled.

"I miss you mum," he whispered, almost under his breath. "I wish you could've seen this."

Breaking the silence, Isla cartwheeled into the room and threw herself on Carson's lap.

"Daddy will be here soon Carson, we need to get ready."

"Does your battery ever switch off?" Carson chuckled. "I'm just having a minute. I still need to tidy this lot up." He gestured around the living room where there was a tidal wave of colour waiting for him.

"I've got an idea – let's see who can pick up the most wrapping paper in two minutes," Carson said, challenging Isla. "Timer is set. One, two, three, GO!"

They both (Isla in her own way) worked tirelessly to sort out the mess from the party. Isla kept stopping to play with one of her new toys or to pop another mini dairy milk into her mouth. 6.30pm came and went and there was no sign of dad. If he didn't show up, Carson wouldn't be able to handle the disappointment on Isla's face. He could see Isla was waiting eagerly for dad. She kept glancing out of the window expectantly. The second hand of the clock seemed to have slowed to an agonising crawl. 6.40pm, still no dad. It was 6.50pm when dad finally arrived.

MOUNT RAINER

"Hey Carson."

Isla bounded towards her Dad and gave him a great bear-like hug.

"Happy birthday darling," Dad said, holding up an envelope which caught Carson's eyes.

"Dad, what's in that envelope?" he asked.

Dad pulled out three tickets as Carson stared. His jaw dropped. He smiled at his dad as he gave him a simple nod of approval. Isla, looking at the envelopes, started jumping and down as if she were a rocket and started racing around the room.

"Where are we going Dad?" Curiosity flooded through Carson.

Dad explained that they would fly to North Washington and watch the sunset above Mount Rainer, which was above the clouds.

"You have worked really hard this year Carson, so I wanted to make Isla's birthday special for the both of you. I...umm...," It looked as if he wanted to say more, but instead he placed his hand on Carson's shoulder and squeezed it: his face an unreadable mask. Dad turned to Isla.

"What do you say darling? Are you up for a plane ride with your old man?"

Carson could see the effect their dads' absence had had on Isla. Her bottom lip trembled. Water started forming at the corner of her eyes as she choked, "I'd love to. I'd love to." Her voice was barely a whisper. More than all of the times that dad had let Carson down, this hurt him the most. He felt a sharp stab in his heart and felt it shatter in that very instance. He didn't realise how much dad's absence had affected Isla. He thought he was doing enough for her. The three of them stared at each other. The silence was deafening. There were a million unspoken words to be said. The silence continued with the only sound being Isla's heavy breathing. Dad was the first one to break the silence.

He cleared his throat. "We had better get going. Our timeslot and pilot is booked for 7.45pm, just in time to see the sunset. You will love it darling - there is nothing like it. Once, your mum and I.." he stopped short. "No time for stories. Let's go," he continued.

***

When they arrived at the airfields, Isla bounded forward, however Carson held her back, trying to contain her excitement. Dad led them towards security, and they each handed in their tickets. Soon after, they arrived at the gate and waited patiently- Isla full of beans. Dad clutched her shoulder as if it were a walking stick. What had this trip meant to dad?

A few minutes passed and a voice announced, "If the Dalton family of three could make their way toward their plane, please. Your pilot, Mr Edmund is waiting to receive you."

Dad boarded the plane and helped Isla in. Carson followed. Carson and dad both went to strap Isla into the leather, padded seat. As their fingers met at the clasp, they glanced at each other before dad quickly removed his hand and stared out of the window. This was the most contact Carson had had with his dad in over two years, but he knew he had to tread carefully; he was desperate for this to be the start of their relationship – how it used to be. Dad used to be so loving.

Once they were strapped in and listened to the security announcement, they were ready to take off.

"Pop this sweet into your mouth sweetie, it will stop your ears from hurting." Isla took the sweet from Carson without saying a word.

***

Looking out of the window, Carson stared in awe at the landscape before him. Everything looked more beautiful from higher up. Mountains seemed to protrude through the tip of the sky as the sun started to droop down. The vast forest below housed dense trees, which concealed many adventures, pleading for people to explore its' many mysteries.

Forty-five minutes later, they were descending down slowly towards Mount Rainier. They hovered above the mountain while dad called over to Mr Edmund, "This is the perfect spot, thank you."

"My pleasure Sir. We can circulate around this vicinity for the next half hour. Enjoy the view with your family."

"I can see it! I can see it!" Isla jumped up and down in excitement.

The sunset was beautiful. Streaked with the vibrant

34

colours of orange and red, the horizon glowed deeply, sending sparks that shimmered in all directions. Silhouetted against the horizon, a silver lining caught Carson's eyes. He tried to make out what it was, but the vision was unclear – almost like there was a translucent film in front of it. Although they were viewing the sunset from inside the plane, there was an electric energy in the atmosphere while they soaked in the beautiful sight that met their eyes. Total silence. As they continued to gaze at the sunset, a strip of golden yellow found its way towards the dominant colours of red and orange: it was like a smile was merging into the horizon, causing the crimson red to shine brighter.

"Stunning." Carson's voice was barely audible. He turned to look at Isla and noticed that she had fallen asleep. A peaceful, calm sleep with a steady rhythm of her heartbeat being the only sound emanating from her little body. It had been an extremely long time since Carson had felt at peace like this – truly at peace. He gazed into Isla's sleeping face and without thinking, stroked her golden locks. Dad was the first one to break the silence.

"I...I..." Dad stuttered as he rubbed his sweaty palms

while he tried to piece his words together. He looked Carson directly in the eye while he continued. " I am going through a hard time at the moment and I understand that you are too". Dad felt a sudden gush of relief wash over him as he had lifted the burden which had cursed him for some time. He was finally able to address Carson. Dad wanted more than anything to try and explain to Carson why he had been acting the way he had since mum had passed. As Carson watched his dad in disbelief, a sudden parcel of fury exploded inside of him.

"UNDERSTAND?! UNDERSTAND?!" A jolt of pain coursed through Carson as his blood boiled and his heart thumped. Dad watched in shock as Carson continued his outburst.

"I am still a child and you left me to deal with everything! With mums' death! With Isla! With everything! Alone. I needed you dad – I really needed you and you weren't there! It was like you also died with mum!" Two years of hurt had built up inside of him and now, like a volcano, it came spewing out like lava. Continuous tears streamed down Caron's face and he was shaking from the combustion.

A long awkward silence lingered in the air. Dad buried

his face in his hands as he had suddenly realised the enormity of what he had done or not done - what he had left Carson to deal with on his own. A silent tear rolled down his cheek. Carson couldn't look at his dad any longer. Panting heavily, he shifted in his seat and turned to face the window. Dad also struggled with the confrontation, but he pushed through his feeling of unease. He had to.

"Carson, son, I am so sorry for everything," his voice cracked as he spoke. "I know I am in the wrong, trust me I realise what I have put this family through, what I've put you through and I deeply regret it." He edged closer towards his son and placed his arm around his shoulder.

"I know it's no excuse, but when mum passed, I...I was in denial – I was angry. I felt my world crash around me and I didn't know how to deal with it. I was a coward Carson. I knew I would have to step up soon, but you managed everything so well, so it felt like I didn't need to. I threw myself into work – anything to keep busy. Do you know how many times I stood at the top of the stairs in the evening wishing I could come downstairs to see you?"

"Why didn't you?" Carson's fury had evaporated as quickly as it came and he spoke in barely a whisper.

"I didn't know what to say. I know that's no excuse. Trust me, you can't hate me anymore then I hate myself. I'm so sorry son and I promise, I'm going to be here for you and Isla if you will have me back in your life?" Dad was now visibly shaking.

Carson could feel his dad coming back. He smiled and nodded towards Jaden as his eyes continued to stream with tears. They both shared a moment as they looked out towards the illuminous moon and its companions: the stars. No more words were exchanged, but Carson could feel everything was about to change. Nothing would bring his mum back, but he could sense that a new family was forming. A family of three. A deep sigh, laced with hope, escaped him.

***

UNEXPECTED

After they had discussed the 'hard' things, dad began asking Carson about his school, his friends, Isla's party. He was desperate to catch up on everything he had missed. While deep in conversation, they hadn't noticed the drastic change in weather, disrupting the calm.

Lightning struck. Dazzling arrows of lightning tore the night sky apart. Above, an immense guillotine blade struck across the horizon. Simultaneously, thunder roared like an earthquake. It then rumbled ominously and crashed and howled overheard. Soon enough, both thunder and lightning collided, creating a catastrophic ambience. This didn't just feel like a thunderstorm, it felt like a thunder-battle.

Immediately, the plane jolted right, then left. In that same moment, Isla's head jerked forward like an arrow and dad, who was sitting next to her, forced her head back with all his might. Feeling slightly dizzy, she awoke with a start.

"C...Car...Daddy," stuttered Isla, remembering dad was next to her. Fear was radiating from her entire body, consuming her.

Dad turned his attention to the pilot. "What's happening Mr Edmund?"

Frightened and panicked, Mr Edmund faced dad – his features contorted with terror. Instantly, dad recognised the terrified look on the pilots' face. A sharp jolt of unease pierced his stomach as panic grabbed his insides, wringing his gut.

"Carson!! Are you strapped in your seat?" Dad almost shrieked at Carson. "Are you strapped?" he howled once more. Carson nodded as he watched on - he could feel panic emanating from dad's entire body.

"What can we do?" Dad almost growled at the pilot, while he was being catapulted from left to right. No response came from the pit of the plane.

As dad was screaming over the roar of the engine and the howl of the weather, Carson stroked Isla's arm, resuming his protective position. "Listen princess, the weather isn't behaving itself. You have nothing to worry about. Everything will be ok. We may just have to land soon. I'll be here holding your hand the whole time." Carson then turned away from Isla as he felt a jolt of ice run down his spine. He couldn't lose anymore members of his family. He wouldn't.

Suddenly, the engine roared ferociously and a stream of scarlet fire shot out from the tail of the plane. Smoke filled the inside of the jet and enveloped Mr Edmund, causing him to completely lose control of the yoke. At that moment, the deafening noise that filled the air was paralysing and the plane began to nose-dive towards the ground. Pressure was building up quickly inside the cabin. The control panel was beeping and the alarm was blaring in warning. Time seemed to slow down around Carson as he could make out his dad's yelling and Isla's screaming. At that moment, a peculiar sensation of weightlessness crashed over him like a tsunami. Life was toying with him. He could feel his lungs clog up as he tried to gasp for air.

He tried to keep hold of Isla's trembling hand, but was finding it increasingly more difficult by the second.

"BRACE POSITIONS ALL!" Mr Edmund bellowed at the top of his lungs as the plane continued to plunge rapidly downwards. "God save us all," he continued in a tremulous whisper.

As the plane continued to plummet recklessly towards the ground, Carson's vision began to deteriorate.

Abruptly, a deafening screech pierced Carson's ears like the heartbeat monitor in the hospital – like his mother's death machine. Everything seemed to be unfolding in slow motion and he felt as if the ground was racing towards him, then suddenly, silence. Everything went black.

When Carson woke, flames were engulfing the plane.

What happened? Where were they? He looked to his left, then right, scanning for Isla or dad. His heart was in his throat and his breathing was like the howling wind on a stormy night. He soon realised that Isla was now calling out his name. As he looked towards the direction of the voice, he tried to inhale deeply.

"CARSON! CARSON! DADDY!" bawled Isla, sobbing uncontrollably.

Without a second thought, Carson leapt up, knocking his seatbelt out of the way and tracked Isla's voice towards the front of the plane. Before reaching Isla, he saw his father trapped under the armrest of his seat, lying unconscious. Blood was seeping from his left leg and he lay there motionless. Carson stopped breathing. He felt nauseous. He could feel his stomach tighten with every breath. He dropped to his knees, head sagging forwards as he began to weep. He clutched at the back of his neck as he spoke.

"Dad...Dad...D," was all he could whisper in-between sobs. Before he could do anymore, he saw Isla watching his reaction and he could feel the heat rising. The fire must be getting closer. He used the corner of his sleeves to wipe his now stinging eyes and forced himself to pull it together.

There was no other choice.

Using all his might, he tugged at dad's lifeless legs and at last managed to pull him out of the prison-like chair. Whilst heaving his father's body from the plane, he also grabbed Isla's hand and as fast as humanly possible, he dragged them out of the burning aircraft. Parcels of panic swam through Carson, however he had to compress this, to squash this emotion; he was used to containing his feelings and now he had to do it more than ever. Blood was dripping from his father's leg, leaving a trail behind them, but he could not tend to that now; he had to get his dad and Isla safely out of the plane before it erupted in flames, killing them all instantly. He continued to struggle towards the fire exit, knocking the door out of the way with his foot. Carson could feel Isla's pleading eyes on him, but he couldn't look at her – he knew he couldn't give her the reassurance she so desperately needed. At last they were out and without a word, he placed his father onto the muddy ground. Isla sat next to her father, calling, no, begging for him to wake up.

"Daddy, Daddy please wake up. I don't want you to go."

Tears were forming profusely in her eyes as an

excruciating pain pierced her heart like a merciless spear. Carson felt destroyed seeing his sister weep like that. Utterly destroyed. He didn't want to lose another family member, not today, not ever. His eyes were stinging as if a swarm of wasps were in them. Although Carson desperately needed to tend to his father's wounds, he couldn't concentrate on that now, he needed to go back and help Mr Edmund. Was he still alive? Was he trapped? Had he been hurt?

"Listen princess, I need to go back to help Mr Edmund, but can I ask you a favour? I need you to be a brave girl for me."

Carson could feel his throat clog up, but he had to steady himself. He had to keep it together. He wondered if putting such a big responsibility on Isla would be too much for her, however there was no other option. Carson wrapped his arms around Isla in the most comforting embrace possible and he felt her sigh into his chest. He kissed the top of her forehead and began to speak, whilst stroking her hair.

"I need you to hold this cloth on daddy's leg. We need to stop the bleeding, otherwise he will become very unwell." Carson choked up on the last word, so he took in a long, deep breath and continued. "Do you understand what I'm saying princess? Can you do this for me while I go to help Mr Edmund?"

Carson pressed the tattered cloth over dad's wound and with his other hand took Isla's and placed it gently on top of his. Isla was visibly shaking, but she took over the compression of dad's wound.

"Am I pressing too hard Carson? I don't want to hurt daddy," she asked. She had a fierce look in her eyes and in that instant, Carson knew he could leave her while he went back for Mr Edmund.

"That's perfect princess. I'll be back soon, I promise." The flames were now rising and Carson was becoming increasingly more terrified. Rising flames was not a good sign. He slipped out of his Nike hoodie, wrapped it around his mouth and nose and securely fastened it behind his head. He re-entered the death trap, stumbling over the edge as he went in.

"Mr Edmund, quick, we must GET OUT!" Carson yelled with desperation in his voice.

He began racing towards the front of the plane and as he did so, he could make out that Mr Edmund had collapsed on the floor.

"SIR, LISTEN, PLEASE!"

Before Carson made it to Mr Edmund, the fire raged on, spreading its wings in all directions, swallowing Mr Edmund's body in its fury. It was merciless.

"NOOOOO!!!!" Carson tried to screech, but no sound came out. It can't be true. Why did he not go back sooner for Mr Edmund? Carson felt sick. He was drowning in guilt. He stumbled to the closest chair and collapsed in it, clutching his chest – he couldn't breathe. He couldn't take anymore. He wanted to sit in that chair and let the fire swallow him also. He was done. Life was cruel and he didn't want to live it anymore. Then he thought of Isla on her own with dad's unconscious body in the middle of nowhere. She must be petrified. Those words lingered in his head for a moment as fresh guilt erupted inside of Carson, before he lurched out from his seat and raced towards the fire exit. He managed to narrowly escape, stumbling onto the muddy ground next to dad and Isla. He was coughing profusely from the inhalation of the smoke.

"W...wh...where is Mr...Mr Edmund?" Isla stuttered.

Carson couldn't speak. He looked at the plane and, in that moment, the flames towered even higher, devouring the entire plane. The windows shattered, causing the glass shards to scatter everywhere.

Isla gasped as new sobs broke out from her chest. Carson took over the compression of the wound. He could barely see from the tears in his own eyes.

"Isla, princess, fetch me the first aid kit over by the tree." Carson was glad that he had grabbed this on their way out. Without saying a word, Isla handed him the red box. Hands trembling, Carson opened the first aid kit and desperately started to tend to his father's wound, which had blood gushing out. As Carson began, the torrential downpour drenched them all and thunder continued to roar. Isla needed Carson, but he needed to wrap dad's thigh in the bandage, before he could figure out what they would do next. The more Carson wrapped the bandage around dad's leg, the more tears formed incessantly in Isla's eyes as she watched on in despair. By the time Carson had finished, tears were streaming down Isla's face like a waterfall. With a hint of panic evident in his voice, Carson attempted to comfort Isla.

Breathing heavily, he wrapped his arms around her.

"Listen princess...,"

Isla interrupted, "C...Carson, what's happened to daddy? He's not dead like mummy, is he?"

Carson's brain abandoned him as he didn't know how to reply to Isla.

"No, princess. Um...um... he's, he's... just sleeping right now, that's all," Carson quickly finished off his sentence. "But let's let daddy rest while we go and get help for him."

Carson looked around, unsure of where to start. It was pitch black. He could barely make out the shadows of the nearby trees. A shiver trickled down his spine, but he had to keep it together. He had no choice. Carson was the only one able to save his family now. Dad lay motionless on the muddy ground, but he had a pulse – this was a good sign. He knew that if he could get help, his dad had a chance of survival. His eyes glazed over as he thought of Mr Edmund. He knew only too well what Mr Edmund's family were about to go through. His throat was thick. He tried to swallow, before looking at Isla and working hard to push these thoughts to the back of his mind.

"Where are we going to find help?" Isla whispered.

After searching his surroundings, Carson made a blind decision to head in the direction where he could hear a trickle of water. That could mean there may be a sign of life nearby.

Carson took Isla's hand and replied as confidently as he could, "This way princess. We are going to find help for daddy."

NATURE'S WRATH

After what seemed like hours of walking through nothingness, Carson and Isla, continued advancing towards the sound of water. The gurgling was now an unpleasant groan; as if it was warning him of the many dangers that were sure to lie ahead. Isla suddenly tripped on a vine, which caught her on the ankle, causing her to stumble towards the ground. She yelped in pain as she grazed her knee on a thorn. Carson tried to grab Isla.

"Are you ok princess?"

Nodding weakly, she murmured, "Yes."

Now clutching her hand, Carson heaved her up from the ground, comforted her, and ensured he had a tight grip on her hand. They continued to walk on the muddy path that Carson could now see as his eyes adjusted to the dark.

Moments later, he spotted a river blocking their way. It was rushing down, every drop racing to arrive at the sea. Carson tried to look for a path around the edge of the river, but it was no use. The river was like a huge curtain of silver. They were surrounded by the smooth glass of water, with the river twisting and turning through the forest.

"Which way now Carson?" Isla asked, trembling.

Carson's voice broke and Isla could hear the trepidation filtering through.

"I think... I think, we need to walk through it. It doesn't look too deep," his voice was threaded with panic.

Carson could see that Isla's face was a storm of fear and exhaustion.

"I'll carry you through it," he quickly added, trying to reassure her.

Bending down, Carson gave Isla his back and asked her to put her arms around his neck before hoisting her up. He then closed his eyes momentarily, took 3 deep, long breaths and began wading through the murky waters. It was cold. Not just cold, freezing. The water stung like a mosquitos' bite. Carson could feel his legs begin to numb and he shuddered.

As he continued forward, he could feel mud squelch beneath him, causing his foot to sink into it. The river wasn't deep, just above his knees, but it felt like a long trek through the churning, grey water. Isla was silent. Carson was silent. The only sounds to be heard were the torrents of the water as they waded through and now the trickling of rain.

Isla had gone limp on Carson's back and he knew from her heavy breathing that she had fallen asleep. Carson was glad of this. Isla didn't need to suffer along with him. He longed to be able to rest. To feel the comforting embrace of protection. He was tired of being the protector. He longed for his mother's touch more than anything. She would've known what to do. Hopelessness washed over him and his face became shadowed with grief and misery. Tears were dropping from his eyes just like the rain from the clouds. Stifling his sobs, Carson swiped at his eyes with the corner of his jumper as his vision was becoming increasingly more blurred. Despite his effort to ignore the cold threatening to consume him, Carson could feel his legs turn to lead and every step forward felt like a battle. He had to win the war. He continued to take measured, slow steps in the water. As he looked up, Carson could now make out the end of the river and a new sense of hope filled his chest. Although the rain was now lashing down, it didn't seem to matter as Carson was nearly through the worst. He adjusted Isla on his back as he began quickening his pace.

Once Carson neared the edge of the river, he held on to Isla while he climbed out of the muddy, slippery slope. He secured one hand on Isla and another on the edge of the squelching muddy bank, which was smeared all over him, as he hauled himself out of the murky water. He was drenched. As Carson attempted to shake off his boots, Isla started to stir, yawning and rubbing her eyes.

"Isla?" Carson said in a dry, raspy voice. He cleared his throat. "Are you ok missy?"

With a trembling murmur, Isla answered, "Where are we? What's happening? Is daddy ok?"

As a ball of dread expanded in his stomach, Carson decided to leave the question about his dad unanswered: it hurt him to think of his dad lying alone in the middle of nowhere, unconscious. He couldn't think of that now – he had to keep his focus or they were all doomed.

"Sshh princess. We just need to walk a bit further. I've

got you."

Once they were out of the murky waters, Carson realised they were on an incline. He looked up. A steep incline. Carson grimaced. He was just so... exhausted. He didn't think he had energy for an uphill trek.

"I need to rest for a moment before we start walking up this." His voice was shaky.

Carson looked at Isla, who was now shivering. She was wet through from the torrential downpour that had attacked them earlier. He sat her down on the muddy grass next to him and hugged her tightly, trying to warm her with his body heat. It was no use - he could feel her quiver. Isla was tucked in under Carson's arm and he gently rested his head on her head. Although they were both freezing and incomprehensibly shattered, neither of them could move. They sat motionless: Carson wondering how much more he could take while Isla praying that Carson would get help for them soon. She knew Carson wouldn't let her down. He never had before. Closing her eyes, Isla let the exhaustion take over. Carson could feel Isla's body relax as she dosed off again. She was completely shattered. At this moment, he began to realise his immense thirst, which was now burning his throat. Each swallow felt like a time ticking bomb; time ticking until death knocked on his door, the door which he thought for certain he would open.

Was there any point climbing this monstrosity of an incline? Where would it take them? Would they even find help?

He looked around at his surroundings and slumped back against the bark of a tree and began sobbing. He doesn't try to stop the tears anymore, he doesn't try to stifle his cries, he just sobs. He has no choice now. His eyes are stinging from exhaustion, or is it from crying? Does it matter? He's near the end now. He doesn't want to continue. He can't continue. He'll be meeting his mum soon. He shuts his eyes and lets the black cloud overwhelm him. Take over. Engulf him. He sinks deeper and deeper into the dark nothingness. He clutches his medal tightly and remembers his mum. He prays for his dad. He takes one last look at his sister's sleeping face. Her trusting face. A sharp pain of guilt stabs at his heart. His mum's dying wish was that he protects his sister at all costs. How can he give up now? But how can he carry on when he doesn't know where he is going? Just then, from the corner of his eyes, he noticed Isla's eyes open slightly, give him a comforting smile, squeeze him tightly and then drift back to sleep. That was the push Carson needed to continue. He could do this. He could do this for Isla. He could do this for his dad. He could do it for his mum. Determined, Carson rubbed his eyes, pulled Isla and stood up.

"C'mon missy, we need to get going. We have left daddy for long enough."

"Huh?" Isla was yawning, however she stood up and took Carson's hand.

"Will you walk for a bit and I'll pick you up again shortly?"

Isla nodded and they ventured forward. With trepidation and adrenaline that he had never experienced before, he took the first step of what was going to be a laborious, torturous climb.

Clambering up the steep hill, Carson could feel the burn in his calves, but he ignored it and kept pushing forward.

After some time, Carson looked at Isla and asked, "Are you alright princess or would you like a piggyback?" He didn't need a reply – Isla's answering nod gave him what he needed. He forced a smile and continued, "C'mere you!"

Kneeling down, he placed her arms around his neck and hoisted her onto his back. They continued their arduous trek up the incline, all the while looking for any signs of human life.

After what felt like several, unbearable hours, they finally arrived at the top. What he saw flooded him with hope as the sun was beginning to rise and he could now see more clearly. Could they find help here? Carefully, Carson placed Isla down and soaked in his surroundings.

Dense fog gathered in the centre of the terrain. They made their way forward, noticing a distinct silhouette in the distance. As they edged closer however, his hope turned to despair as he noticed the silhouette he had seen was in fact a house, which stood dilapidated and abandoned - the fog slowly creeping towards it; tendrils, like fingers, clawed their way closer, slowly smothering the open pathway that led to the entrance of the house – the oak door shrouded.

"Do you think someone lives there?" Isla asked, full of hope.

"I...umm...I...Let's go closer."

Carson noticed the frame of the door had a corner missing, all splintered and fractured from where the mites had been gnawing for what looked like centuries. Each screw had its own swarm of mites, chewing from corner to corner, fighting and competing against the rest. The metal on the door handle had eroded with rust and the colour had faded from the harsh gold that it once was to a dull grey. For a brief moment, Carson was lost in this world as he took in what lay ahead of him. Isla gulped as she noticed the debris lying around. The broken pieces of the once loved home now shattered into a million pieces. Crammed, intertwining trees swarmed the area like bees, providing a canopy, which was protecting the house. The trees look downwards, raising their status above. Leaves scurried along the path and the breeze became keener, causing goose-bumps on Isla's arms.

Towards the back of the house, Carson could make out gravestones, which stood stationary, helpless and crippled from age - each symbolising its life through the gentle glimmer of fight that was shining softly from above. The wind howling - almost creating sounds like the whispers of those who lay beneath. No other sounds could be heard except the soft footfall of Isla and Carson as they stepped across the moss-covered ground, exploring further. All around, the dead were kept company with statues of mythical creatures and gargoyles, who were perched comfortably against the old black, wrought fence – its' spikes covered in old vines.

Stone angels peered in as if to keep intruders away, or perhaps to invite them in and numerous black cats roamed around each and every grave as though they were there to pay their respects. Isla shuddered taking in the sinister-looking graveyard that lay behind the house. Carson rubbed her shoulder and turned her gaze towards the house.

"Should we see if it's open?" He held Isla's hand and they edged closer; all the while, Carson keeping Isla slightly behind him with a protective arm in front. Carson placed his palm over the greying doorknob and it turned with a click. Pushing their way in, the oak door creaked in protest as Carson forced it open.

There was no light in the house - the laughter of the children that once occupied the house had died along with the light of the day. In the darkness, the bleak hallway was unwelcoming. Upon the walls, Carson could make out photographs of children, once obviously so loved, however were now covered in a blanket of dust and cobwebs. The floor, which was once an old-fashioned parquet with a blend of deep homely browns was now snaked with a blueish, green mould. The banister was a twirl of a branch, tamed by the carpenter's hand.

"This house would have been beautiful," Carson whispered almost inaudible, his breath visible in the bitter chill.

"H...hello...?" Carson asked, clearing his throat.
It was no use. This was clearly a house that had been left to rot years previously. He could see how uncomfortable Isla felt in the house, so he led her back out. At this, her chest fall, just as her hope left her body. Carson straightened up.

"Come on princess. Don't worry, we'll find help soon."

"Are you sure? Is Daddy still waiting for..." she couldn't finish her sentence as panic and uncertainty flooded through her.

"Very," smiled Carson with conviction. "But first, I think we need to rest a little. I've walked through the night, so I just need a sit down before we continue. Let's build a small den to shelter us from the wind."

Isla nodded and watched as Carson bent down to pick up a couple of logs. They twisted and grated against each other like rusty hinges. The logs pressed on him on all sides, causing scratches down his left leg. He ignored this, saw the perfect spot for a den and ambled towards it. The area Carson had spotted provided a canopy of trees in which he could build their den under for extra shelter. Walking back and forth, Carson collected the branches and placed them under the cover as Isla watched on.

"Are you just going to watch me missy?" he joked, trying to lighten the mood.

Isla burst out laughing. Carson was the one person in the world who could make her laugh any time. Before he could speak again, Isla was running off, attempting to collect branches.

Panting, she struggled to lift the branch she had stopped at and called Carson. He rushed over to her to see that she was having difficulties with the branch.

"It doesn't want to come with me," Isla whined, continuing the joke.

Chuckling, Carson helped her – together they carried it to the den area.

Once they had gathered all of their twigs and branches, they began to build the den. They started off at the back.

There were a few twigs that couldn't keep still, sticking out in all directions. They used this as a back wall, which would help shield them from the wind that was now getting stronger. The walls were full of various creepy-crawlies; Isla made a face at these. Isla and Carson, clearly focussed on the den building task, enjoyed the respite from thinking about dad's motionless body alone. Their mind needed this break.

After some time, the den was steady enough to provide shelter for Carson and Isla to rest in.

Stepping inside, Carson bent his head and took off his Nike hoodie – which was now dry from the murky shallows earlier and placed it on the rough grass. Isla had already crawled inside and was excited by their little 'den'.

"It's so much warmer in here Carson," Isla exclaimed.

"That's because we can't feel the wind princess," Carson replied with a yawn. "Anyway, come lie down next to me, let's rest for an hour or two and we will be fresh when we wake up."

Carson opened up his arms and Isla snuggled into him. She was so exhausted that she fell asleep almost instantly. She had always felt safe with Carson. He looked up to the sky, sighed and tears once again started rolling down his cheeks. Now that he didn't have to pretend in front of Isla, he was consumed with grief. Mr Edmund had died because of him. He knew he could've saved him if he had acted sooner. If he was just a few minutes earlier, Mr Edmund's family wouldn't need to go through the mourning that he has faced these last 2.5 years. He hoped it wouldn't tear their family apart like it tore his. Mr Edmund's family would be completely unaware of the tsunami that was about to be released upon them. That would engulf them. Then he had the added guilt of how long he had left dad for. When they left, dad was still breathing even though he was unconscious, would he still be breathing now? He had to be alive. Carson had to believe this – it was the only thing forcing him to continue – to find help. He rubbed at his medal, which was still in his pocket – it went everywhere with him as a sort of protection. Carson's eyes were burning as if they had molten lava. He knew in that moment, that if he wanted to save his family, he needed to have some time to sleep. He hoped he wouldn't be too late. Continuous thoughts whirled around in his mind as he drifted off into nothingness, into darkness. Finally.

HOPE

It was the early morning birdsong that awoke Carson from his slumber. It was a calm, overcast day. The sunless sky covered the woods over the treetops, which created a canopy over his head. The crimson and auburn foliage was a magnificent sight, bringing Fall to life. There was a gentle breeze, creating the sound of rustling leaves. The leaves appeared as though they were dying to fall out of the tree and join their companions on the forest floor. Together, with pine needles and other flora, the leaves formed a thick, springy carpet. The forest was pure and clean, as though it had never been disturbed by man and his vicious, life-killing machines. Peacefully sleeping under the dark-grey sky, the community of mighty timber had not a care in the world.

Carson rubbed his eyes and looked around at his surroundings. Where was he? He stretched and rubbed the back of his neck, trying to gather his thoughts. Then realisation dawned on him like a tsunami. He was in the monstrous hellhole which the devil himself had engulfed him in – that place with the merciless and unforgiving wildlife. He jumped up in panic and looked for Isla, who he noticed was stretched out on the ground next to him. His mind was working at 100 miles an hour and he knew that he needed to come up with a plan before waking Isla and continuing their rescue mission. The sleep was good for Carson as he now had a clear head and was able think without a cloud shrouding his thoughts. His stomach was grumbling furiously and he knew that Isla would be starving the moment her eyes opened.

Just after Carson had thought of food, Isla awoke, moaning and groaning.

"Caaaarsonnnn!" she bellowed. "Where are we? I'mmm hungryyyyy!" Her bellow had scared off a flock of pigeons who were peacefully resting on the bark of a willow.

"Calm down missy!" exclaimed Carson, tying up his wavy, dark brown hair. "We'll try to scour for some food."

Isla, excited by the mention of food, tugged on Carson's arm before leaving the den and running off ahead of him into the wilderness of the woods.

Now jogging to catch up with Isla underneath the shade of the trees, Carson found himself appreciating the scent of pine needles: the ambiance of autumn. Encompassed by the thick heavy air, Carson watched as a single sparrow fluttered high above the emerald forest. A few feet next to him, an eager squirrel hastily scampered from tree to tree, awaiting the chill of winter. The forest, he realised, was home to many wild creatures. In giving protection and food, the forest was gladly rewarded with the company of these animals. Beyond the horizon, Carson could see the community of newly formed saplings. They appeared as little children, learning under the guidance of their grown and fully matured parents. Suddenly out of the corner of his eyes, he could make out a berry bush.

"Hey, Isla, look what I found," Carson said, trying to manage a smile.

Isla scurried over and without hesitation, grabbed a few dozen from the finger-like, untouched branches.

"Woah hold on there missy!" exclaimed Carson, grabbing Isla's hand. "They might be poisonous!"

Carson examined the potentially harmful berry. What if they were poisonous? But Isla was painfully hungry. He hated to see her suffer like this, like a stray animal scavenging for food.

After a few more seconds of hesitation, he carefully placed

the purple coloured berry onto his tongue and started to chew ever so slowly. Tasting. Feeling. Thinking. Isla watched, waiting. Soon after Carson had tasted the berry, he noticed the sour bitter after-taste lingering in his mouth, however no harm had been done to him - yet. He decided they would be safe for both him and Isla to eat. It had been at least twenty-four hours since either had eaten and he knew Isla couldn't cope for much longer without food.

"Carson Carson!" she shouted with a hint of excitement somewhere in her voice, "Can I eat them, can I eat them?" Her emerald, green eyes twinkling, whilst she jumped up and down. Carson had no idea where this surge of energy had erupted from.

Without answering, Carson held out his hands with the wild berries he had picked, and allowed Isla to pounce at them, causing her face to be smothered in the sticky, sour juices from the fruit. After she had eaten them, she scoured around her surroundings, her once twinkling eyes now filled with hunger – she felt like her stomach was a bottomless pit, however she couldn't see any other berry trees to satisfy it.

"Isla, why don't we have a look down there?" Carson indicated further along to where the thicket of trees blocked the scenery. "I think there could be some more berries there," he continued, darting towards the dense trees.

Isla pelted after Carson at full speed, causing her to collide into him. He gripped onto her hands and together they inched deeper into the wilderness.

"This is beautiful, Carson," Isla gasped.

"It feels like we are locked away from the world under the protection of these trees, doesn't it?"

"Daddy would've loved this. Like mummy."

"Don't give up on daddy princess, he's going to be ok. We have to think happy thoughts. Close your eyes for a moment and open your hand."

Carson placed a handful of juicy berries in her palm. "Open your eyes now princess. Look at how alive these berries are, how fresh they are. We must be close to help now."

"But..."

"No buts missy, enjoy these berries and then we will get

help for daddy. You must keep your hope alive in here," Carson continued, pointing towards Isla's heart.

Carson was trying to convince Isla as much as he was convincing himself. If he let the dread take over, it would render him useless. He couldn't afford to wallow. He clung onto hope as if it was the only thing left in the world.

After Isla had finished the berries, she noticed a grove of trees swathed in them. Instantly, she attempted to grab one - not waiting for her brother to test them first. She couldn't reach them. As Carson reached up to pull the branch down, Isla looked ahead and saw... footprints. Life.

"Carson, look, look, footprints," Isla exclaimed, her face lighting up as she jumped up and down, almost stepping on one of the prints, which were imprinted on the muddy ground.

Carson instantly let go of the branch he was holding

and faced Isla.

"W...W..." Carson was stunned into silence. "Come here you little monkey," he almost chuckled as tears rolled down his cheeks. Happy tears. They hadn't found help yet, but he could feel it was close. If these were old footprints, they would've been washed away with the rain. Someone was here this morning. Carson could feel his breathing getting heavier as he began to pant. He couldn't believe he was going to get help soon.

"Carson?" Isla was cautious now, edging towards him.

"Hey, hey, I'm ok princess. Careful. Make sure you don't step on the footprints. It could lead us to help. For us, and for daddy." He hugged Isla in a tight embrace, almost smothering her and looked up to the sky.

"I'm going to save her mum. I've kept my promise," he whispered in a murmur. It felt like the weight of the world had been lifted from his shoulders.

"What did you say?"

"I said I love you. Now let's follow the trail!"

Carson scanned the area to where the footprints led to. He noticed more prints ahead - but this time, pawprints. He grabbed Isla's hand and yanked her towards them. In front of him, lay a muddy path with a mixture of the prints. Carson's heart soared and he felt as if it would burst out of his chest. He couldn't help the tears now flowing rapidly down his face as he walked towards the path with a new-found conviction.

The pulsing beat of his heart became calmer as he exclaimed, "We've done it, we've found help. We can save daddy. You have saved us princess."

Isla looked to where Carson was gesturing: she could make out a clear path which was previously concealed by trees. The path, which was leading in the opposite direction of where they had slept, was covered in prints. They had done it.

Isla let out a squeal of delight as Carson hoisted her onto his shoulders. They were both consumed with elation and were becoming increasingly giddier by the minute.

"You look ahead princess. You are our Satnav." He began to hum as they ventured towards hope.

Filled with increasing contentment, however still a hint of worry embedded deep inside of him, Carson walked with a slight pace along the forest path. Despite the many intersections, which appeared frequently, swerving off into many wonders of the hidden forest, Carson tried to avoid his curiosity taking over; he continued to stride forward, tunnel vision - as if it were a single walkway leading to either impending doom or eternal hope of rescuing his father. Carson's legs were moving automatically, as if they had a brain of their own. The sounds he could fathom were the crispy sound of the leaves, their footsteps and distant hooting and howling sounds, however overpowering all of these, was the pounding of his heart: the constant anxiety. Carson kept moving, with a lurking fear bubbling at the pit of his stomach – what if their hopes were crushed? What if these footsteps were a fraud? Carson couldn't think like this. He had to keep his spirits up. They would find help. Clamping down on his fear, he surged forward.

"Carson are you ok?" Isla asked tentatively. "Why are you so quiet?"

Carson let that question ponder for a few moments.

"Yeah I'm ok, I was just looking ahead," he managed a smile. "Don't be such a worry-pot!"

Giggling, Isla exclaimed, "I'm not a worry-pot, you are – you always go quiet when you're worried!" They both laughed – the ambience of hope searing through the air.

All of a sudden, the crisp leaves beneath their feet softened. Carson and Isla felt as if they were walking over sand. Not dry sand, but the slimy sand. It was almost like the ground of a marsh. Carson was praying all the while that this wouldn't be the end of his trail, and with each prayer, his intensity grew. The footsteps were now lost under the gooey mud.

Carson's Airmax trainers started dipping in the gunk, which was occasionally touching his uncovered ankles. He moved his legs until he could move no longer. Carson's legs were numb from the chill; it was snapping viciously at his bare ankles. He lifted his face, letting the light and shadow dance across his skin. Although he shuddered under the intensity of the cold surrounding his legs, he was glad to feel that Isla was ok on his shoulder. Isla looked above and noticed a scurry of squirrels scuttling across the side of the pathway, as if scavenging for nuts. The soft crunch of them on the ground made Isla wistful. They were a faded, shredded tapestry of autumn, she thought as she remembered when she, her mother, her father and Carson would venture out on the fresh autumn evening. Many memories came back to her as the leaves danced, pirouetting from the naked trees in a shower of colour, bringing a warmth to the biting chill that was beginning to settle in.

"Hey Carson, look there, squirrels!" said Isla, breaking the silence.

"And another - look up there princess, there's one!"

"Wait, where, where?" A smile of wonder and curiosity formed on her face. Looking towards the isolated scurry, Carson rubbed Isla's legs, which were dangling in front of him. He wanted to protect her from the bitter chill that was threatening to consume him.

"Aww, look at that one, I wonder why he's leaving his family."

"Come on missy, we have a mission to fulfil."

Isla tore her eyes away from the scurry and on her right, she could make out the lush evergreen trees, which were standing firm, as if the roots were clinging for their very life. In the distance, there was a crystal, clear river. Carson could hear the rampaging rapids, which slowly converted into a swift river forcefully turning at every bank. The river cut through the middle of the woodland and diverted into another as a tributary. After what felt like hours of walking across the never-ending pathway, Carson could feel himself going insane, having thoughts he wished had never crossed his mind. Gruesome thoughts. Disturbing thoughts. He wondered if his dad was still alive. He wondered if his dad would still be breathing. He wondered if his dad had woken up and was looking for them. He wondered what Mr Edmunds' family must be thinking. He wondered if they would've sent help to look for him. The thoughts bombarded him like missiles. He felt sick, until he noticed something. A light. His heart skipped a beat as he squinted his eyes to make sure it wasn't a mirage. Help he thought.

"Look Carson, look Carson!" Isla exclaimed haughtily. "A light, Carson we did it, we did it."

They continued to walk on: Carson pulling at his sleeve as Isla grabbed hold of her brother's neck. Soon they came to an Inn where a black door stood tall. Carson gulped and swallowed in with equal measures of fear and excitement as his eyes drank in the sight.

THE INN

Carson lowered Isla from his shoulders, and instinctively placed a protective arm in front of her. He edged forward cautiously and tapped the door, gently at first. His voice was laced with panic as he called out, "Hello, anyone there?"

No answer. He knocked a little louder this time. Still no answer. Tears prickled Isla's eyes as her hope threatened to be crushed. Carson's heart sank, but he couldn't give up, not yet.

With all his might, he budged the door with his shoulder. Simultaneously, a bearded man with a flat cap opened the door, causing Carson to stumble in. Isla hovered at the threshold.

"'Ey matey, you a'righ' there?" Seeing the distressed look plastered on Carson's face, he added, "Need some 'elp?"

"Yes, yes please," Carson panicked. His words exploded out of him like a tsunami. "My dad's back there... Mr Edmund didn't make it... we are lost... we don't know where to go... I don't want my dad to die.... I." He was cut off by the stranger.

"Calm down, me ol' chap. Tell me the whole story. Take yer time."

Carson took in a deep breath. He held Isla's hand tightly as he began by telling the man how his dad wanted to take him and Isla to view the sunset on Mount Rainier. Carson explained how their plane crashed violently, sending destruction everywhere.

"Who's Mr Edmund? Is 'e the man who, umm, died when yer plane crashed?" The innkeeper interrupted. "Sorry, I've no even introduced meself, how rude. I'm Ronan by the way, but you can jus' call me Ron. All me friends do."

"Yes he is," answered Carson.

"Look me ol' chap, the little lassie must be freezing and you both must be hungry."

Ronan bent down on one knee and took Isla's hand. She edged behind Carson and looked down, biting her lip.

"It's ok princess." Carson rubbed her shoulder reassuringly and brought her forward.

"How about we take you to sit by the fire? Do you like dogs? Mylo can keep you company and I can give you a woolly blanket to keep you warm while I talk to yer brother here. You have nowt to worry about lass. Nowt I tell you."

Isla nodded, unable to speak. Carson led Isla to the fire and Mylo came bounding forward. Isla laughed as the husky danced around her and then sat next to Isla by the fire. She patted his head with caution at first, before ruffling the hair on his body more enthusiastically. Ron handed the blanket to Carson, and he draped it over Isla. Gently, he stroked her hair, kissed her forehead and then turned his attention back to Ronan.

"Jake!" Ron called out to the back kitchen.

"Hola," came a reply from afar.

"Put together somethin' warm for me friends, would you. A nice hearty meal."

Ronan turned his attention back to Carson.

"Can ye' describe where yus were when the plane... crashed? That will help me locate yer dad. I know these woodlands like the back o' me hands."

Ronan knelt down beside Isla again. "Don' worry me love, we'll find daddy in no time."

Carson watched Isla relax and relief washed over him as he knew they would find their way back to dad. He had full faith in Ronan. Sighing with relief, he realised that they weren't on their own anymore. They had support. He had support. The question was, would dad still be alive when they got back?

"Oh ho, look what me pal rustled up for yus!" Ronan exclaimed as he rubbed his palms together with a cheeky grin when Jake came out with a tray of food.

"Thank you Ron, but I really think we should be starting our jour..."

"You need to keep your strength up. 10 more minu'es won't hurt." Ronan nodded deliberately in Isla's direction and Carson could see how utterly exhausted she was. She needed all the strength she could muster before venturing back out into the cold.

Carson nodded reluctantly.

"As soon as you've polished that lot off, I'll get me truck. I know which direction yus came from. Hopefully it won't take us more then a couple o' hours to get back to yer dad."

Carson nodded.

"Isla, look what this lovely man has brought out for us. Come over to eat," Carson exclaimed, walking towards Isla.

Without thinking, Isla jumped up from the sofa, startling Mylo, who had his head resting on her lap. Isla rushed over to the wooden bench and table, where Jake had laid down the food. Mylo, hot on Isla's heels, was sniffing and wagging his tail. He had clearly smelled the food also. When Isla saw the feast before her, her eyes popped like popcorn. Ron handed out the plates, and Carson spooned the stew onto Isla's plate. He added some fluffy potatoes and a handful of vegetables from the mixture – asparagus, green beans and baby corn. Silently, Isla dug in straight away, hoovering bites in without waiting for her mouth to be empty before the next bite entered. Carson watched her and realised how hungry she must've been. Guilt stabbed at him – a few berries weren't enough to eat in over twenty-four hours. She must've been starving. But what else could he have done? He took comfort now, knowing that she was eating to her hearts content and he lifted the spoon to serve himself.

They ate their meal in silence; the only sound was the constant chewing of food and the scrapping of their forks on the plate. Carson had never tasted stew so delicious. He hadn't eaten stew in over 2 years. He could feel the warmth of the steak melting in his mouth.

"I've brought out some drinks to wash yer stew down

with," Ron said, emerging from the kitchen. "Coke for you and squash for the lass, that ok?"

"Perfect, thank you. Can we also have some water? Tap is great. It's been a while..."

But before Carson could finish his sentence, he and Ron both looked over to Isla, who had gulped down the glass in one sip. Ron smiled.

"Let me refill that for you love and I'll bring out some water also."

Soon enough, both Isla and Carson had eaten to their fill – even devouring seconds. Once finished, Jake came to grab the plates from them, as Carson smiled at him appreciatively.

"Cheers mate, that was perfect. Just what we needed." Carson said to him, his eyes full of gratitude.

It was now time to make the journey back. Back to dad. Carson had never been so grateful for another human as he was for Ron right now. Ron had fed them, dried off their coats and was taking them in his car to recue his dad. Carson could feel tears prickle his eyes – he couldn't contain his emotions.

"Hey, hey, matie, we'll get to yer dad in no time, don't

worry me ol' chap."

"I... just... thank you. I'll never be able to repay you," Carson whispered weakly, tears now flowing.

Ron rubbed Carson's shoulder and Carson could feel the care and concern in that small gesture - his hope soared. They would be with dad in no time. He just knew it.

THE JOURNEY BACK

As Ron revved the engine in an attempt to start the car, Carson noticed a scent of the moist evening dew cascading all around the sublime forest. The mixed cool autumn leaves from the tall trees lay scattered on the forest floor; they were in the motion of turning a brittle brown. The crunch was emphasised as Ron drove over them, pushing their papery remains deep into the soil which lined the ground like a newly placed tarmac. The isolated forest remained in a capsule, untouched by the destructive essence of man. Isla stared out of the window, taking in the passing sight, while beginning to rub her eyes.

"Hey, you okay princess?" whispered Carson, aware that Isla was drifting off to sleep.

"Yeah I am," she said yawning, still rubbing her eyes.

Moments later, Isla was asleep, breathing heavily and leaning on Carson's shoulder. He smiled down at her, grateful that she was getting more rest.

"Sleep princess, sleep," he murmured.

Carson looked straight ahead and noticed that the dark

shadows of the trees and bushes had become the structure of the forest. The trees stood proud and tall like protectors of the exigent grounds, as the bushes that had consumed the hard regions of the forest, concealed the land from beneath the vibrant portals of the open sky.

As Carson could now appreciate this wonder from the warmth of Ron's truck, he sensed that the isolated forest had the appearance of autumn romance which blossomed, alluring his mind deeper and deeper into the enchanted land.

He soaked in the beauty as he watched the sun rise in a timely hurry, as if trying to make up for setting so early the evening before. The sun bloomed into the sky with a warm mellow glow, sending what was left of the sun packing until his next stint overlooking the day. The dusky sky was a brilliant bright orange and yellow, which perched picturesquely on the autumn branches of the trees in the forest below. Isla was now snoring loudly and as Carson absorbed the calm view, he gently caressed her hair.

"It's beau'iful out 'ere, isn't it?" Ron asked seeing that Carson was mesmerised by the sight before them.

"Yeh. How long have you lived here for?"

"Ooh, maybe comin' up for 22 years. I can' see meself in a city. This is where me 'eart is."

Carson merely nodded, ending the conversation. He was utterly exhausted and this wasn't helped with his mind oscillating between the wonders of the forest and the crushing thoughts of his dad. A knot of dread formed in Carson's gut when he thought of dad, but he tried to squash these thoughts. He inhaled deeply and began concentrating on the countless jewels that lay before him.

The mellow sun set over the reflective lake. The sheen of reflection on the arctic water from the glowing sun sparkled in the tranquil air, with the light reflecting unique combinations of blue hues and pearlescent purples. The only sounds to be heard were the chug of Ron's car and Isla's heavy breathing.

As Ron continued in the direction of where he believed the plane had crashed, he reminisced about his twenty-two years away from the city and about how his land was isolated from the prospects of busy city life. Undisturbed. He loved that the immense trees possessed a sweet serenity that kept him safe in the forest from stark human impact. As thoughts were whirring around in his head, Ron looked over to Carson and noticed his sombre expression deepen. Ron gave him a gentle nod.

"Ye' alright pal?" he said in a comforting tone.

"Yes... I am thanks," replied Carson, managing a fleeting smile.

"If ye' don't mind me askin', whereabouts is ye' mum?"

Taken aback by the question Carson stuttered. "I... Uhm," he choked at his words.

Now realising the answer to his question, Ron comforted Carson. He took one hand briefly off the steering wheel and rubbed Carson's shoulder.

"It's a'right mate, say no more."

Just then, in the distance, Ron spotted what seemed to be a beacon of grey lingering ahead. They continued in the direction of the beacon until they became enveloped in the smoke.

As it obscured his vision, Ron abruptly stopped the car, causing it to almost tip on its' side. Isla woke up startled and confused.

"What happened?" she asked, alarmed at the sudden stop.

"Don't worry princess, we're here now." Carson's voice

was filled with hope and anxiety.

Now eager to find dad, Carson swung open the door, and swivelled out of the car in an attempt to search for his father - his pupils were dilating.

"CARSON, CARSON!" yelled Ron. Carson, alarmed by Ron's yelling, turned back, however then he noticed dad's silhouette and started running in the opposite direction, to where he had left his dad forty-eight hours earlier - his heart was pounding and his eyes were tearing up; the chilly wind biting at his face. He could now see his father clearly - his pale lifeless face. The dried blood smothered across his head. Carson's heartbeat intensified. Isla stood there, shocked, mortified, and hopeless - tears filling her eyes. Ron had taken her to Carson and she crouched down next to her dad.

"Daddy, daddy, please wake up," she whispered as she held his hand. Carson hated seeing Isla like this, he was meant to help her, like how he had promised his mother, however right now, it wasn't about Isla, it was about his father.

Now crouching down as well and feeling for dad's wrist, Ron could feel a faint pulse, however a grave expression cemented his face.

"We must call 911," Ron said in a low voice; he seemed hopeless, and his once lively personality changed to a sombre demeanour. He grabbed his phone from his back pocket and immediately dialled 911. Carson could hear the conversation.

"911, what's your emergency?"

"Yes, we have an unconscious man here, his pulse is very low, please send help I don't think he can be here much longer."

"Right away Sir, just hold on for a bit. Where is your location?"

"We are at the coordinates 46.8 degrees North and 121.8 degrees West of Mount Rainier."

"Ok, one moment. Yes. We have your location. I'm sending a team out straight away."

"Thank you. Thank you."

"Can you tell me what happened to the man Sir?"

"He was in a plane crash with his son, daughter and a pilot. The pilot is...no more."

Carson's lip began to tremble at the mention of Mr Edmund. What would his family be going through right now? What would they go through for the rest of their lives? Why couldn't he have saved Mr Edmund? He had blood on his hands and he knew it. He shook his head, trying to clear it. He had to stay focussed for now. He had to lock these thoughts away – he was used to pushing his emotions away, so he should be able to do that now.

"Ok Sir, we will need the details of the pilot and of the unconscious man please."

Ron looked over to Carson, who nodded and gestured for the phone.

"Hi, I'm Car...Carson. I was in the plane with my dad when it... crashed."

Carson finished the conversation with the operator, giving full details of the crash and his dads and Mr Edmund's name.

Once Carson had finished the conversation, he buried his face in his hands and began to weep. Really weep. He was both relieved and terrified - mixed emotions coursing through him. Too much was going on, he couldn't handle it. Isla had gotten up from where she sat next to Ron, who had been comforting her. She tugged at Carson's hand. He let go of his face and began to hug Isla so fiercely. Both were now sobbing. They couldn't tell if it was because they had finally managed to get help for dad or if it was because they were afraid that they had been too late. Ron walked over to the siblings and placed a hand on both of their shoulders.

"Hey, hey. It's going to be ok. Your dad, daddy..." he said, addressing Isla, "... is going to be alrigh'" He tried to smile convincingly.

Ron was looking directly at the bandage that Carson had originally wrapped dad's leg in, which had now become drenched in blood. A crimson carpet cushioned dad's leg. Ron let out a breath of air. He didn't know their dad, but he knew that there was no way Carson and Isla could lose another parent – they wouldn't survive it. They were barely holding on by a thread now as it was.

"Listen mate, I've an idea, why don't you and the little lady wait in me jeep. It's freezin' out 'ere. It will..."

Carson cut Ron off as if slicing through the air with a blade, "I am not moving until my dad moves. I am staying with him." He felt shear panic at the thought of having to leave his dad again and his throat became clogged as he began to inhale. His face was set in stone.

"I know, I know, it's ok mate, it's umm, jus'," he continued in a whisper, "Isla is freezing, look at her, she's shiverin'. She needs you mate," he pleaded.

Carson nodded, then sighed in defeat. Opening the door, he picked Isla up and helped her inside the back seat of the jeep. Mylo bounded in after them, brushing passed Carson. Mylo wouldn't leave Isla's sight, almost as if he had taken on the role of her protector. Carson followed next and gestured for Isla to sit on his lap.

"When will the ambulance men come to help daddy?" Isla asked.

"Soon princess. You have nothing to worry about. You can rest on me until they come. Try to sleep."

Fifteen minutes later, Mylo started gnawing at the door and Carson opened it before he chewed off the handle. He lurched out of the car, barking. His nose was pointing towards the direction of a whirring noise.

"Wha's up?" Ron began to ask before hearing the noise himself. "Good boy, good boy." Ron was now almost laughing.

Carson caught on, grabbed hold of Isla's hand and dashed out of the jeep. They began to watch as the helicopter came closer. Carson looked up to the sky.

"Sorry mum, dad isn't joining you yet," he murmured under his breath, clutching his golden medal.

"It's landing!" Isla shouted over the whirring noise, covering her ears.

As soon as the ambulance landed, a calm chaos rained upon them. Three paramedics rushed out of the helicopter. Two towards dad and one towards where Carson, Isla, Ron and Mylo stood watching.

"Hi, I'm Julie, one of the paramedics here to assist you today. Are you ok?" She glanced between Isla and Carson, who clearly looked like they had been dragged through the mud. Ron intervened.

"They've been through a lot these past forty-eight hours.

I'm Ron by the way. They ended up at me Inn for 'elp. This is Carson and his little sister, Isla."

Julie smiled comfortingly at Isla and crouched down. "Are you hurt darling?"

"Will daddy be ok?" Isla answered instead.

"Over there, tending to your daddy are two lovely paramedics called Davey and Albert. They are going to do everything they can to make sure your daddy gets what he needs." Julie nodded in the direction of where the two paramedics were working on dad. They didn't look as calm and in control as Julie was.

"Pulse yet?" One was shouting over the whirring of the helicopter, while incessantly pumping dad's chest. The other paramedic, Davey, felt dad's pulse on his wrist.

"It's weak. Get the mask on him. We don't have much time."

Albert placed the mask over dad's face and nose, meanwhile Davey started to attend to dad's leg. He looked grave.

"He's lost a lot of blood. Too much. We need to get this bandaged up and get him to a hospital ASAP." Davey shouted as yet more wind roared. "Pass me the gauze - it's on the right."

Julie looked back at Isla. "You see, they are trying to make your daddy safe for flying honey and then we can all go to the hospital. Now, are you ok? Have you been hurt anywhere?"

"My left shoulder has been sore since the crash."
Carson looked down, ashamed of himself. He hadn't even asked Isla if she was hurt, not really. He only had a single-track mind - to find help for dad. His bottom lip began to quiver and Ron patted him. Ron could feel Carson drowning in guilt and he had no reason to.

"Listen mate, you saved her. I would be very proud if I had a son like you. Your dad is a lucky man."

"Ok, let's go and sit in the helicopter..." Julie started.
Isla looked panicked.

"Carson will come as well," she continued, "And we will have a look at your shoulder and see if Carson needs help too."

"I'm fine," Carson interrupted. "Let's get Isla sorted."
Once in the helicopter, Julie started to feel her way around Isla's shoulder.

"Tell me where it hurts honey."

Once the check was complete, Julie turned her attention to Carson.

"I'm certain nothing is broken, it feels bruised. I'm happy to say that I think she will be ok in a few days with regular use of an ice-pack, resting it and paracetamol."

"Thank you," Carson breathed, exhaling.

"Now, Carson, can you tell me what happened while I write down some notes. I'm sure Davey and Albert won't be too much longer."

Carson explained how the flight had started, then gave details of the crash and the fire and Mr Edmund and their journey to the Inn. Whilst he was recalling the events, Julie was jotting down notes, her face soaking in all the details.

Near the tree where Carson had laid dad, Davey and Albert had now stabilised him and were ready to transfer dad onto the stretcher.

"Alright!" yelled Davey over the sound of the roaring helicopter as Albert was holding dad by the head. "On the count of three, we lift him up!" he continued.

"Yes sir!" bellowed Albert, now crouching down holding dad by the head.

"3...2...1!" With a heave, they hoisted dad onto the

stretcher, strapped him in and began to pick the stretcher up as gently as they could. Carson was somewhat in awe at how they worked so efficiently, he always wanted to be a paramedic; he remembered how he and his mother used to play doctors with each other.

"Hey, ye okay mate?" Ron called to Carson, bringing him back to the present.

"Yer father is gonna be ok ye know," said Ron tentatively. Carson smiled. He was reassured by Ron's words- he felt safe with Ron. "Well, I suppose it be time for me to leave. Yer in safe hands now."

"Wait, what?" Carson's smile morphed into a surprised look, "Why can't you come?"

"I'm no family, I would'na be allowed. I've also gotta take care of the Inn of course!" He tried to cheer up the mood. "It 'aint gonna run by itself."

"Yeh, don't worry I understand," said Carson, upset that Ron wouldn't be able to travel with them. They had become a team. He wasn't sure what he expected, but with Ron there, Carson finally felt like him and Isla weren't alone, making it hard to say goodbye.

"Hey, how about we swap numbers? Sound good?"

"Yes, that will be great. And, umm... thank you for well... everything." His voice was full of gratitude and appreciation.

"You've got nothin' to thank me for matey. Just doing me duty. Let me know how yer dad is doing when you are able to."

Carson nodded, and with that, Ron and Mylo climbed back into the truck, and waved before driving off.

Now focused on dad, Carson, who had goosebumps erupting like a volcano around his body, watched as dad was put in the middle of the helicopter. Julie, who was now holding onto Isla's hand, nodded towards Albert, indicating that they can start the 40-minute journey. Isla was covering her ears, trying to sensor out the noise. Julie provided Isla with a pair of Hello Kitty earmuffs to help her; she smiled in return.

Carson looked out of the window, and before long, they were on their way – in the air once more. Isla was next to him and he noticed her immense exhaustion.

"Hey missy, you okay?" he said, still looking down at her. Isla looked up, fatigued and barely able to turn her head. Isla couldn't make out what Carson was saying due to the loud whirring noise from the helicopter. He repeated himself louder this time.

"Yes, I'm ok Carson, just tired," she said stifling a yawn.

Without thinking, Carson gently cradled Isla's head, laid it on his lap and started stroking her head comfortingly.

"There you go princess, try to catch a few minutes of sleep before we get to the hospital."

Within minutes, Carson could hear the faint snores of Isla sleeping. Now that she was sleeping, he could let the worry engulf him - he turned to dad and whispered, "Come on dad, you can do this, not much longer- I know you can. Hold on for us."

Julie noticed Carson's panic and squeezed his shoulder. His answering smile was weak. His heart was heavy, his mind was fatigued, his body was aching and he was more exhausted then he had ever been in his life.

"We'll be there soon honey, you should try and get some rest also." Carson nodded, more out of politeness – how could he possibly sleep now?

THE HOSPITAL

Before long, the helicopter had arrived at the St Gutherie hospital and Carson witnessed several paramedics rushing out with various sorts of machines and equipment. Davey and Albert rushed out of the ambulance and on the count of three lifted dad up. Isla immediately awoke with all the commotion around them.

"Over here boys!" yelled a gruff man, motioning towards an entrance, which read 'Accident and Emergency'. The siblings were escorted by a young man into the hospital. Isla was holding dad's hand the entire way, until they were separated. Dad was taken into a private room and Carson and Isla were asked to wait in the waiting area. Julie followed shortly afterwards.

"How are my two favourite people holding up?" Julie smiled.

"What's the plan from here?" Carson asked, too anxious to play along.

"The doctors are now going to assess your dad and see what they can do to make him better. I assume he will be put on an oxygen machine to start off with and I imagine he'll definitely need a blood transfusion, given the amount of blood he lost from his leg."

Carson's face morphed into panic.

Julie quickly continued, "This is all perfectly normal and will help your dad. They will then assess what else they need to do and a doctor will come and explain things to you as soon as they can."

"Thank you. You have been very helpful," Carson replied.

"I need to head back out shortly, but before I go, would either of you like some toast?" asked Julie, with a warm smile. Knowing Isla was probably hungry, Carson gave a quick nod and Julie was on her way towards the back room. Moments later, Julie reappeared with two plates of toast, and placed them on the table.

"I better be off now, but if there is anything you need, ask Nurse Maria, she's on duty in this area." And with that, Julie glanced down at her pager and backed away from the room.

"Go on Isla, eat, you'll need the energy for when daddy wakes up."

Without hesitation, Isla started eating the toast. Once

she had finished, she turned her attention back to Carson.

"When are we going to see daddy?"

Just then, a doctor with spectacles and a white coat entered the room.

"Hello you two, I'm Dr Byron. I have been treating your dad."

Carson's face lit up. "Yes doctor, what is it? Is dad going to be ok?" The doctor explained that he was still working on dad, but the first thing that they needed to do was a blood transfusion.

"Ok, is dad going to be alright?"

"I'm afraid it's too early to say just yet, but I wanted to keep you in the loop every step of the way. We are doing everything we can. I promise. Try and get some rest and I'll be back when I can with some news."

"Please save my dad, doctor. He's all we've got," Carson pleaded.

"I will do my best."

As Carson watched Dr Byron leave, he felt a sharp pain pierce his gut. He felt like he could be sick. Why hadn't the doctor said dad was going to be ok? Why couldn't anyone tell them dad would make it out of the hospital alive?

They waited for what felt like an eternity. They waited for the doctor to bring them good news, they waited for the doctor to tell them that dad would be ok, they waited and waited.

"Princess, why don't you sleep for a little while? Come and..."

"No, I want to be awake when the doctor tells us that daddy is going to be ok," Isla retorted with a solemn expression.

"Listen princess, the doctor is a busy man. He has lots of patients to make better. When he comes into the room, I will wake you up."

"Promise?" Isla tried to stifle her yawn, but gave in and nodded.

"Promise missy. Now come on my lap and rest your head."

Carson embraced Isla and with that, she was off. He wrapped his protective arms around her and began stroking her golden locks – although they weren't so golden at the moment. Carson could also feel his eyelids droop, but he forced them open. It felt like hot needles piercing his eyes, but he couldn't give into it. He couldn't remember the last time he had had a good night's sleep – he had lost track of days, but all he knew was that he had to be awake when they came to give dad's fate. *Their* fate.

A couple of hours later, Dr Byron entered the waiting room. Carson instantly jumped up, too anxious to remain seated.

"Hey!" Isla started to protest at the sudden jerking, but then laid her eyes on Dr Byron and hid behind Carson.

"I'm sorry to have kept you waiting," Dr Byron began.

"Please, tell us Doctor," Caron's eyes were pleading.

Dr Byron couldn't contain his smile, "Your dad is going to make it."

Before Dr Byron could say anymore, Isla burst into sobs. "Can I see daddy?"

"One moment princess, let's hear what Dr Byron needs to say."

Carson turned his attention back to Dr Byron, who continued, "The blood transfusion was successful and so was the operation. Your father is heavily sedated to help with the pain, so we don't know how long it will take for him to wake, but he will. I promise you, he's going to be fine."

Carson knelt down beside Isla, and they both began to shake, tears streaming down their faces.

"Daddy is going to be ok princess, we saved him. We are a team, me and you - always!"

"When can we see him Doctor?" Carson asked, turning his attention back to Dr Byron, who was already receiving messages on his pager for another emergency.

"Give us fifteen minutes to sort the room out and then you are welcome to wait in his room. I really must be going now. Sorry."

"No, no, that's absolutely fine. Thank you so much for all of your help Dr Byron. Thank you."

And with that Dr Byron made his way out, leaving Isla and Carson embracing each other. Neither could speak, they merely hugged, both lost in their own thoughts.

"I think we should start making our way to daddy's room," Carson breathed, tearing himself away from Isla. She nodded, suddenly looking wary.

"Hey, hey, what's the matter? Daddy is going to be fine."

"Will he look different after the operation?" Isla managed to ask.

"That's what you are worried about?" Carson's lip

twitched at the corners into smile. "Daddy will still look like daddy, now come on."

He took Isla's hand, gently swept her hair from her eyes and led her out of the waiting room. As they walked through the long corridors, Carson felt uneasy. He could hear the cacophony of panicked voices and beeping from various rooms - with each beep, he could feel it jab at his chest. He tried to quicken his pace.

"What's wrong Carson?" Isla whispered, while Carson was practically dragging her forward.

"Umm... nothing, I'm just eager to get to daddy," he replied, his face vacant.

Just as they neared dad's room, another doctor, Dr Damen, emerged from inside.

"Hi, I'm Dr Damen, you must be Isla and Carson?"

"Yes, yes, has something happened?" Carson's voice suddenly rang in alarm.

"No, no. We were just clearing the room. It's all sorted now. Dr Byron told us we would be expecting you. Please do go in. Your dad is absolutely fine. You are welcome to wait as long as you like."

"Thank you."

"I'll have Nurse Maria bring you over some refreshments once you are settled. It could be a long wait."

Carson smiled at Dr Damen, gripped Isla's hand tighter and slowly began opening dad's room door. As soon as Isla saw dad, she bounded in and was about to jump on dad, before Carson caught hold of her hand, yanking her back.

"Woah missy, daddy needs us to be extra careful with him."

With that, Carson edged forwards and sat at the chair by dad's head, taking dad's hand; he remembered the warmth it provided him when he was young. He inhaled deeply and tried not to notice the unsightly machine dad was plugged into. He tried not to notice the stale hospital smell he could so clearly remember. He tried to focus solely on dad.

A tear rolled down his cheek as he looked towards dad and pleaded, "Dad... I... really need you to get better. I need you." He tried to swallow back more tears, while Isla's eyes were fixed on him.

"Please, please, wake up. Please dad. You promised me you would be there for us." Carson felt hot drops rain down, brushing against his cheeks. "I need you, I can't do it on my own anymore," he whispered as he broke down. He let go of dad's hand and let his head sink into his palms. His head was pounding with every tick of the clock. Carson regretted the time he shouted at dad on the helicopter, he regretted being moody with dad on Isla's birthday when dad hadn't noticed the decorations, he regretted not talking to dad sooner after mum, he regretted it all. Although they knew dad would wake, the waiting felt like forever.

"C...C...Carson, daddy is moving his eyes!" Isla almost screeched after some time.

As Carson looked up, he noticed Dad's eyes flickering. Unsure what to do, Carson yelled, "DOCTOR, DOCTOR!" Instantly, two nurses raced in. Isla was now in tears, shaking dad's arms in an attempt to wake him up faster. One of the nurses had removed the oxygen mask; it seemed like the exact same mask which had killed his mum. Mixed emotions coursed through Carson like daggers whilst he took a few steps back, allowing the professionals to examine dad.

"He won't be needing his mask anymore, his oxygen levels are fine," one of the nurses said after analysing the machine, a warm smile spreading over her face.

"It's nearly time for your dad to wake up. You can hold his hand and wait by his bedside, so he can see your beautiful faces first when he wakes," the other advised, squeezing Isla's shoulder.

"Thank you," said Carson, the black cloud beginning to dissipate.

The nurse gave a warming smile, nodded and left the room carrying the oxygen monitor with her.

A short while later, Carson noticed dad's eyelids slowly opening

"DAD, DAD!" Cason exclaimed.

The sound of Carson startled Isla, causing her to jump up out of her seat. Dad, who was groggy, gazed around with a mask of confusion painted across his face.

"Where am I? What happened? What's going on?" dad croaked, looking around at his surroundings. His hesitant eyes slowly opened.

"I'm here. It's Carson. It's okay dad. Everything is alright." Carson blurted out, trying to reassure him before he started panicking. "Even Isla is here with us."

Carson took dad's hand and looked him straight in the eye, giving him a weak smile.

"Do you remember anything?" he asked his dad cautiously.

All of a sudden, everything flooded back to dad - all the memories of the past few days.

Panic suddenly rang in his voice. "The helicopter crash! Are you ok? Where's Isla? Are you hurt? How long have I been in here?"

Carson was taken aback by the torrent of questions. Isla rushed over next to dad and sat on the side of his bed.

"Daddy, I'm ok. We were so worried about you. I thought you were going to go to heaven like mummy." Isla's voice choked on the last words as an abundance of tears began to rain down on her face once more.

"Hey, hey darling," dad soothed, wiping her tears with the back of his hand and stroking her hair. "I'm ok my baby girl and oh, I'm so glad you are here with me. Are you hurt darling?" Isla shook her head, not trusting herself to speak.

Dad pulled Isla in for a closer hug and Carson watched on while the two embraced – Isla had not looked this peaceful in days. She smiled contentedly, her heart soaring. She hadn't been able to hug dad in so long. She breathed in dad's scent and sighed deeply. Although he mainly smelled of the hospital, she could make out dad's scent underneath and she had missed it. Carson wondered if Isla had missed dad these last few days or had she missed him these last few years when he hadn't been around. Her hug was deep and Carson felt his chest heavy, experiencing all of Isla's emotions. It was like there was a wire connecting both of their hearts and he could feel Isla's every beat.

From the corner of dad's eye, he noticed Carson gazing on, although lost in a whir of his own thoughts. Dad motioned for Carson to join the reunion. Carson took a hesitant step forward. He was desperate to have his dad back, but he couldn't allow himself to get hurt again – he simply couldn't take it anymore.

Dad noticed Carson's mixed emotions, which were plain to see on his face, and began, "I'm really sorry about what happened in the flight. I'm sorry I said I will try harder and it didn't go as planned. I'm sorry I let you down, yet again my darling boy." Jayden couldn't finish what he had planned to say and burst into tears.

Carson had not seen dad cry so much, not even when mum died. It was like his emotions, which had been frozen for more than 2 years, had melted and there was now a river of tears. Carson couldn't bear to see his dad like this, so vulnerable, and rushed over. Dad enveloped Carson in his arms, who also began to sob. He had not felt this protective embrace for years. The last hug he had received was from his mother the day before she died. At that moment, Carson knew everything was going to be ok. Dad had remembered his words on the flight and he was back. Isla and Carson had their dad back. They could never get mum back, but Carson could accept a new family of three. A family where Isla had her daddy and her brother watching over her. Maybe Carson could start enjoying time with his friends again. Maybe he could start back at his football club with his dad attending the matches. So many possibilities. His heart skipped a beat, thinking about the future.

"I'll always miss you mum, but we are finally going to be ok – I can feel it," Carson whispered inaudibly, looking up and smiled.

A FEW MONTHS LATER...

"Come on, boy! You've got this!" dad bellowed over the roaring crowd.

"Will Carson get another medal like this one daddy?" Isla asked, rubbing the golden jewel-encrusted coin that was around her neck.

"If you cheer for him, he definitely will." Dad replied, pulling Isla closer to him, while fixing her sun cap. "Shall we shout it together darling?"

At this moment, Carson tore past them, dribbling the ball like a thread weaving between his opponents, his eyes fixated on one place – the goal.

"Yeeesssssss Carson!!!!!!! Scccoooooooorrrrreeee!!! You can do this!" Isla screamed in a deafening voice.

For a fleeting moment, Carson took his eye off the goal and found the place where the voice echoed from. He saw the gleaming locks of his beautiful sister flying in the air, his dad by her side – he smiled.

Swerving past his last opponent, Carson looked at his target once again, the win in sight.

Everything went silent, the crowd a blur.

"This is for you mum!" Carson murmured, smiling as he took the final shot.

The crowd...*erupted.*

ACKNOWLEDGMENTS

First and foremost, I'd like to extend my thanks to Mefuza, who has been with us every step of the way, supporting Khaleel during his weekly writing sessions and ensuring he kept to his timescales.

I'd also like to thank my husband, Aslam, who went out of his way to help us make our book a reality. He believed in us and helped us with the designing stage, pushing the book along. Thanks as always to Esa and Rayyaan, the younger brothers, who showed excitement from the very start and were eager to be our first readers. Our biggest cheerleaders.

A huge thanks to Rachel who took the time out of her maternity leave to be our editor, whilst doing it extremely passionately (and with a fine tooth comb!)

Thank you to Ameena for eagerly awaiting our next chapter to give your seal of approval, whilst falling in love with our characters also. And thanks to Saif, who is always trying to find ways to help promote our book.

I'd also like to extend my thanks to my mum. I love your blinding support in everything I do and this was no different. Thank you for your belief in me, always.

I'd also like to thank my friends who have encouraged me from day one and every step of the way since. Each bit of feedback or encouragement you have given has always meant so much and I'm glad to have you all in my life: Nazmin, Safeera, Harvi and my Dovelanders.

Thank you to Himanshu, our designer, who has spent countless hours bringing our dreams to reality. Thank you for being patient with us!

I'd also like to thank Aisling Fowler, who was busy in the promotion of her own book, yet she took the time to read our manuscript, providing detailed chapter by chapter feedback, which was invaluable. Thank you to Zohra Nabi and Aisha Busby for also taking the time to read our book and for providing beautiful quotes. Much appreciated.

And last, but by no means least, a huge thank you to all of our readers. Every book that is purchased and read is a dream come true.

SOFIA MOTI

grew up in Scotland and loved exploring the beautiful
outdoors with her family. She enjoyed playing badminton
competitively and with the encouragement of her dad,
took part in many county competitions.
After moving to Leicester, Sofia studied at The University
of Leicester to become a teacher.

Currently, Sofia is a tutor, who is passionate about
inspiring her students to aim high and helping them
to find their wings. This is where the story of 'Survival'
comes in. Sofia is immensely proud to have been able to
share this experience with her student Khaleel and her
first-born child, Ameera.